To all those who want to be
hippie grandmothers—including me!
R. L.

To my mom and dad.
A. C.

First edition 2003

Library of Congress Cataloging-in-Publication Data

Lindbergh, Reeve.
My hippie grandmother / Reeve Lindbergh; illustrated by Abby Carter. —1st ed.
p. cm.
Summary: A young girl describes all the things she likes about her grandmother,
including the purple bus she drives, growing vegetables,
picketing City Hall, and playing the banjo.
ISBN 0-7636-0671-5
[1. Grandmothers—Fiction. 2. Hippies—Fiction. 3. Stories in rhyme.]
I. Carter, Abby, ill. II. Title.
PZ8.3.L6148 Hi 2003
[E]—dc21 00-037964

2 4 6 8 10 9 7 5 3 1

Printed in Italy

This book was typeset in Tapioca.
The illustrations were done in watercolor and gouache.

Candlewick Press
2067 Massachusetts Avenue
Cambridge, Massachusetts 02140

visit us at www.candlewick.com

My Hippie Grandmother

Reeve Lindbergh

illustrated by

Abby Carter

CANDLEWICK PRESS
CAMBRIDGE, MASSACHUSETTS

I have a hippie grandmother.
I'm really glad she's mine.
She hasn't cut her hair at all
Since nineteen sixty-nine.

I live in town on Pleasant Street
With Mom and Dad and Russ,
But Grandma lives behind the hill
And drives a purple bus.

She has a cat called Woodstock,
A fish named Tiny Tim,
And a boyfriend with a big mustache.
(Her boyfriend's name is Jim.)

She has plants on every windowsill.
Green vines grow in the shower.
There are posters in her bedroom.
They say LOVE and FLOWER POWER!

I help her in the garden.
We hoe the peas and beans.
We eat cracked-wheat-and-honey bread
In bare feet and ripped jeans.

We're at the Farmer's Market
By noon each Saturday.
We sell some bread and vegetables,
And some we give away.

Granny's JAMS

Sometimes I go with Grandma
To picket City Hall.
If nobody comes by, she says,
"Guess we can't win 'em all!"

At night she gets her banjo out
And Jim gets his guitar.
We sing the song "Amazing Grace"
And wish upon a star.

The moon shines in the window.
The cat purrs at my feet.
I curl up warm and fall asleep
On a psychedelic sheet.

My mother is a lawyer.
My dad works on TV.
My grandma says someday I'll find
The perfect job for me.

She says I could be President
Or go to outer space,
Or find the cure for cancer
And save the human race.

I tell her there's one other thing
I really want to do:
 "Become a Hippie Grandmother,
 So I'll be JUST LIKE YOU!"